Puffin Books

Editor: Kaye W

Pleasant Fieldmouse

Pleasant Fieldmouse really was very pleasant indeed, just like his name. He was always trying to serve the community by being a fireman or organizing a specially nice picnic or good things like that and, when the ladies were anxious over some little mishap like their homes burning down, he was there to put their minds at rest. He was altogether a most helpful, comforting person to have around. When things were at their very worst, he used to say, they were bound to get better next, and how right he was.

As it happens, Pleasant Fieldmouse was a mouse of action as well. He was the one who saved poor Mrs Hedgehog, the best worrier in the world, from Fox's cooking pot, and rescued the mother squirrel from the cage. In fact the name *Brave* Fieldmouse might even have suited him better.

Jan Wahl has packed an enormous amount of friendly, sturdy character into the diminutive figure of Pleasant Fieldmouse, and Maurice Sendak's enchanting illustrations help us to *see* him as well. And as for his poor old oak tree home that got burnt in the fire, many of us will be finding him snug corners in our hearts that will do just as well.

For children of five and over.

Pleasant Fieldmouse

by Jan Wahl

pictures by MAURICE SENDAK

Puffin Books

Puffin Books,
Penguin Books Ltd,
Harmondsworth, Middlesex, England
Penguin Books,
625 Madison Ave., New York, New York 10022, U.S.A.
Penguin Books Australia Ltd,
Ringwood, Victoria, Australia
Penguin Books Canada Ltd,
41 Steelcase Road West, Markham, Ontario, Canada
Penguin Books (N.Z.) Ltd,
182–190 Wairau Road, Auckland 10, New Zealand

—

First published in Great Britain by World's Work Ltd 1969
Published in Puffin Books 1976

—

Copyright © Jan Wahl, 1964
Illustrations copyright © Maurice Sendak, 1964

—

Made and printed in Great Britain
by Richard Clay (The Chaucer Press), Ltd,
Bungay, Suffolk
Set in Monotype Ehrhardt

For Ingrid,
who knew him always

Contents

I am a Fireman   9
The Picnic Which Wasn't   19
Hedgehog Pie   28
The Lucky Button   43
The Guest in the Rose   55
A Forest of Ashes   65

I am a Fireman

The bright sun, the pride of spring, popped into the sky like a flying orange. The forest stirred, then morning began, shaking its new green shades. Red robins and green finches darted among the trees like bold-painted arrows.

Somebody was hammering a sign beside the thick black oak. This somebody was Pleasant Fieldmouse, who lived inside the oak, at the bottom. I AM A FIREMAN it said on the sign. Pleasant Fieldmouse was wearing a fine red hat which was really a cap from a bottle. *Tipsy Cola*, the cap was labelled, but you were not supposed to look at him from the top.

Pleasant stepped back, rubbing paws cheerfully.

'That will let them know I'm in business,' he told himself, since he believed that everybody ought to work at something.

He had a fire wagon, which Haunted Beaver (followed constantly day and night by a whirring, lovesick bee) had promised to pull.

And a net for people to jump in, in case jumping was needed.

And a fly-swatter with a broken-off handle, for beating out fires with.

He felt tremendously prepared. His nose twitched, awaiting the smell of fresh smoke.

'Where are the fires?' asked Pleasant Fieldmouse, scuttling from one far end of the forest to the other, cautiously watching out for Terrible Owl and Tired Fox – who was probably, but not definitely, asleep in his log after running out all night.

'Where are the fires?' he repeated enthusiastically.

However, nobody knew.

Not Greybeard Tortoise. Nor Haunted Beaver. Nor Mrs Worry-Wind Hedgehog, who was too busy worrying that Tired Fox might catch her anyhow.

'Heaven help us, we don't want any!' they all cried, going their ways, though Greybeard Tortoise didn't go his very quickly.

'I'm here to put out fires!' the field-mouse called in his most hopeful, business-like voice.

'Great! Great! Great!' replied Never-Doubting Frog, falling with a splash straight off his lily pad. Yet 'Great!' was all he ever admitted about anything.

No fire licked upward, no smoke rolled across the broad sky.

'Oh, what a slow beginning,' Pleasant

shrugged to himself. He was terrifically anxious to serve the community. When you have picked your occupation, after giving it long, long thought, it is vexing to find there are no fires for you to put out. He thought of starting a tiny wisp of a fire himself – just to practise with – then decided that would be improper. Besides, in the forest, or any place, nobody wants a fire. There is nothing worse, nothing feared more.

So he scanned the horizon (which was hard to do – not only was he small, but the horizon was cluttered with brambles and weeds and bushes and wild flowers and spearlike thorns, not to mention trees, plus the Rabbit family out for a stroll, and so forth), hoping to discover the first trace of smoke in order to put his equipment to use.

He polished his red bottle-cap hat and got ready to sit and wait like firemen do. Should he, perhaps, reletter his sign with brighter paint?

Then suddenly he saw it through the trees: a patch of grey, twisting and curling and changing shape, coming closer every second.

'Fire!' Pleasant Fieldmouse yelled, ringing a whole batch of tin bells.

Haunted Beaver came, huffing and puffing, faithfully tugging the fire wagon which was quite impressive. The bee, as usual, had not returned to its hive but kept flying around and around the beaver's head. 'Where?' Haunted asked, wide-eyed.

'Over there!' said Pleasant, pointing to the grey smoke, and jumping aboard.

'FIRE!' went up the cry. The swallows dropped their berries and twigs to carry the message forth.

FIRE! FIRE! FIRE! FIRE!

'Make way!' Pleasant Fieldmouse announced like a captain, importantly. 'Fireman coming!'

Everybody stepped aside when the splen-

did fire wagon whizzed by, heading into thick smoky clouds which were pouring out.

The only trouble was, it wasn't smoke at all and it certainly wasn't fire.

It was an approaching army of grasshoppers determined to gobble up all the forest leaves, stripping trees and bushes bare.

Dark-grey swarms of them whirred through the air, greedily.

'FIRE!' voices on every side of them were bawling.

At that, the grasshoppers looped back and forth. If there's anything they fear more than the rest of us, it is fire.

'Let's move out of here,' they whispered among themselves.

Just beyond, Pleasant was raising his fly-swatter, preparing – like the hero that he was – to beat out the flames.

'Smoke, I'm not afraid of you!' he cried, stretching to his full height, brandishing the swatter handle.

Haunted Beaver's mouth hung open in

awe. He stood, obedient though nervous, hitched to the wagon.

The forest folk hung back, waiting to see their fireman at work. And then, in a flash, the cloud was gone. The grasshoppers fled in terror from the fire which didn't exist.

Pleasant was pleased, though vastly puzzled.

'I didn't know it was so simple,' he declared. 'I guess you have to be *scary*.'

He rode home in triumph. Some of his admirers piled the wagon to the brim with snapdragons and violets and parsley. He proudly smiled, waving his fly-swatter aloft.

The crowd cheered. A few among them turned cartwheels and somersaults. The wagon, pulled by Haunted Beaver, rattled back down the lane and, dipping at the hollow where the path bends and turns towards the big black oak, went out of sight.

And that is how Pleasant Fieldmouse got his reputation for being a fire fighter.

The Picnic Which Wasn't

The broad gurgling stream which dangled out to the lake and back, making an island out of the forest, was fun to wade across. You hopped from stepping-stone to stepping-stone, and held your nose, in case you fell in.

It was in the midst of hopping across the blue surface – springing from one moss-covered stone to another – that the field-mouse got the inspiration to hold a picnic.

It was the beginning of May. The weather was neither too hot nor too cold.

'In fact, it is pleasant,' he decided, hopping eagerly onto shore, where on the sand he sat, and with a sharp stick drew up plans.

'I'll invite only *good* people, because they don't cause trouble. There is always somebody you want to avoid. If everybody comes, you don't enjoy yourself, I do believe.' Then he sighed, because it was a very sad truth.

Pleasant was more than happy putting up signs. Therefore he made a fine set of them.

INVITID

GOOD PEEPLE (ONLY)
TO A PICNIK
MEET BY THE BLACKBERRY SWAMP
BUT STAY AWAY,
TERIBLE OWL & TIRED FOX
& OTHERS LIKE YOO!

The signs were so high and wide, and he had to letter so many, that it took two days and his paw got very cramped. However, at last they were done and he piled them in the fire wagon, and Haunted Beaver helped him scatter them through the forest. Then home he rushed to construct fancy paper hats and other things required on picnics: mud-fudge (not to eat, just to look at – there was no chocolate anywhere), gooseberry and raspberry sandwiches, Gramma Field-mouse's watercress cakes, and sour root-ade. A delectable feast, he felt sure.

Thus he got ready and tied up the sandwiches in neat parcels with ribbons of grass. Then all of a sudden he knew he had left out something and went hurrying from poster to poster, scrawling under the bottom line, in yellow-coloured letters – since no other kind of paint was left – TUESDAY, although the manner in which he spelled it was TOOZDAY. He was only a fieldmouse, so his spelling left something to be desired – but it looked very pretty in yellow paint.

The forest animals and birds soon read the sign, particularly the part that said

GOOD PEEPLE (ONLY)

and that made them think a lot.

Mrs Hedgehog worried. 'I don't suppose that can mean me. I'm never thinking about anybody except myself, since I worry over me, night and noon. Therefore, Mother of Hedgehogs, without a speck of doubt I know I'm not invited.' The poor lady could

not help worrying. Worrying was inside her, under her fur. And she worried herself off into the wind, wondering if she had left the front door open so Terrible Owl might swoop inside and be there to greet her!

'Great! Great! Great!' croaked Never-Doubting Frog, reading. Though, in his heart of hearts, or a trifle lower, in his stomach, he was aware he had snapped at too many fat flies and couldn't possibly eat at a picnic without severe indigestion.

You cannot be good and a glutton both. He didn't doubt that; so he knew *he* wasn't invited.

INVITID
GOOD PEEPLE (ONLY)
TO A PICNIK
MEET BY THE BLACKBERRY SWAMP
BUT STAY AWAY,
TERIBLE OWL & TIRED FOX
& OTHERS LIKE YOO! TOOD-DAY

Haunted Beaver also studied the sign
proclaiming the picnic. He shook his brown
head, causing the single-minded bee to
grow dizzy.

'Positively, it does not mean me,' he said,
remembering that on the day before, when
he was chewing a white birch tree to keep his

24

teeth sharp and gleaming, the birch crashed, nearly demolishing the schoolhouse. Miss Possum was pretty upset. She was in the middle of teaching Rules of Safety, and screamed, just before the jolt, 'Our forest is falling – is falling to pieces!' She tried to climb into her desk.

Greybeard Tortoise scratched his beard upon a rough stone, thinking, too, about what goodness was.

'I'm so slow and old I make everyone believe he has hurried too fast, and everywhere I'm invited I spoil the festivities. I suppose I had better stay away. I'm sure I am not invited.'

He wheezed and dropped a single tear on the stone, recalling one Christmas party when he arrived after it was finished.

They all slunk off in different directions, not one of them feeling *good* enough to attend.

However, Pleasant sat at the blackberry

swamp on Tuesday upon the high grass, his cakes and sandwiches heaped into nice square piles. For everybody, there were hilarious caps and crazy bonnets, some of them with bright feathers the birds had dropped.

He sat and sat till the day went pale, till the sun sank and a strong breeze blew, blowing long grass ribbons off the sandwiches. A plateful of radishes went rolling down the hill into the swamp.

Pleasant sat smiling firmly, in case somebody showed up – though nobody did.

'I said Tuesday, sure enough,' he whispered to himself, then trotted to the nearest poster to make certain.

Then he returned and fell into a half doze, because he was weary from all that preparing and waiting. Beetles and caterpillars soon scuttled forth to have a feast. They couldn't read, and didn't question whether *they* were good or not. Gramma Fieldmouse's cakes were the first to go. The mud-fudge turned out better than Pleasant suspected.

When he awoke, the food was gone. The beetles had marched home groaning, dragging the remaining radishes to chew at leisure.

'The picnic must have been a huge success!' observed the fieldmouse with delight. 'I only wish I hadn't slept through it!'

Blissfully he gathered up the empty plates. He put the funny hats away. 'It must have been a stupendous picnic. Everything's been licked clean.'

And he trotted home, whistling loudly.

Fortunately no one ever dared to tell him. And that is how Pleasant Fieldmouse gave, or to be more precise, gave away, his picnic.

Hedgehog Pie

One night, when only the moon crept through the crowns of tall trees and almost everybody in the forest was peacefully snoring, two shadows talked together.

The first shadow had a long bushy tail and short sharp ears, and if a light had been turned on, you would have recognized it as Tired Fox. The other was covered with feathers, and grabbed onto a low limb with quick steely claws. It was Terrible Owl, who often shot through the dark air and asked his terrible flying question: 'Who are YOO? Who are YOO? Who are YOO?' And whoever was out walking scurried home to safety, slipping under warm covers.

Now it happened that a long time ago Terrible Owl had made up his mind to catch Pleasant Fieldmouse and plunge him in a stew, but the fieldmouse was always too sly and too fast and seldom ventured out at night. In the strong daylight Terrible Owl was half blind and had to swim through a sunny fog.

However, Tired Fox, whose feet generally ached from long, difficult chases (difficult since the forest was full of popholes – those are holes to pop into – and full of secret chinks and slippery caves just right for escapers to hide in), had come across a recipe for Hedgehog Pie. Actually it was Chipmunk Pie, but he was willing to substitute ingredients.

Mrs Worry-Wind Hedgehog, the world's best worrier, was so constantly afraid of getting caught that she would dance out of her house like a spinning top, watching out in all directions.

So it was that the two would-be cooks got together. 'You help me, I'll help you,' suggested the clever fox. They shook a paw and a wing; and the moon hid behind a cloud.

Soon after, Tired Fox let it be known he was going on a trip. 'I'm going on a trip! I'm going on a trip!' he would casually sing, skipping up and down the path, waving a flag. When the great day arrived, he left by canoe, and everybody saw him merrily off. Up the stream he floated, singing still. The forest folk gorgeously celebrated.

All except Mrs Hedgehog, who worried.

The only good fox
is a fox in a box,

her grandmother used to say, and her grand-mother was considered to be wise.

So Mrs Hedgehog continued spinning like a top, glancing every which way. And as for Pleasant, he continued to keep one eye peeled on the trees for the sudden appearance of Terrible Owl, who might spring fiercely from a bough.

When night fell once more, the canoe slid quietly back down the stream. Tired Fox had rested up on his trip, which proved to be, simply, around the corner and into a little fern-hidden cove on the lake. Altogether he was a trifle hoarse from so much loud singing while leaving, and his fingers throbbed from playing his homemade mandolin. The two shadows once more crept together.

Mrs Hedgehog came out sleepwalking, a rare occasion for her. Pleasant had emerged to pick a pawful of flowers at the other end of the lane.

'Who are YOO?' Terrible Owl politely asked the wandering lady.

'Why, I'm me,' Mrs Hedgehog declared, waking up. 'You know very well who I am.'

She looked up at the branch where the owl sat busily stringing a pretty necklace of leaves.

'Who is it for?' Mrs Hedgehog couldn't help inquiring, beginning to feel that the forest was much improved now that the fox was away.

'Oh, for whoever wants it,' the owl said, finishing it and dangling it fetchingly.

She started to reach for it, blushing with thanks, when out of the shrubbery in which he had been hiding leaped Tired Fox, pouncing upon her and dragging her off towards his log.

'I should have known!' Mrs Hedgehog wailed. 'I should have worried more!'

At the other end of the lane Pleasant dropped his flowers. He dashed along the path, following the fox's red coat and Mrs Hedgehog's frantic arms. The least he could do, he decided, was to bite the fox's heels. Perhaps then the she might wriggle loose.

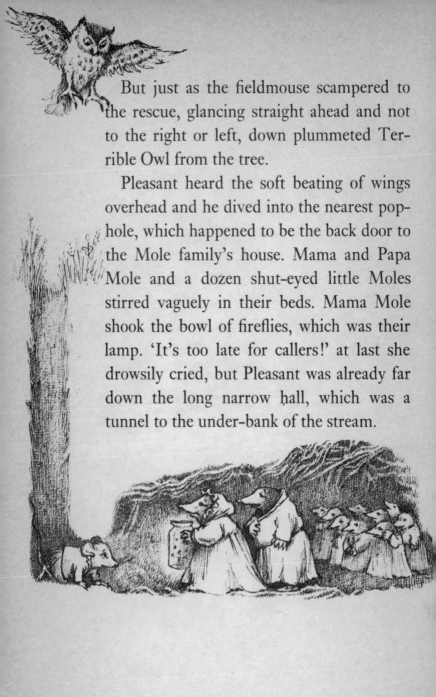

But just as the fieldmouse scampered to the rescue, glancing straight ahead and not to the right or left, down plummeted Terrible Owl from the tree.

Pleasant heard the soft beating of wings overhead and he dived into the nearest pophole, which happened to be the back door to the Mole family's house. Mama and Papa Mole and a dozen shut-eyed little Moles stirred vaguely in their beds. Mama Mole shook the bowl of fireflies, which was their lamp. 'It's too late for callers!' at last she drowsily cried, but Pleasant was already far down the long narrow hall, which was a tunnel to the under-bank of the stream.

He squeezed out from a tiny opening, then peered over the top of the bank. Tired Fox was struggling along the path with his heavy burden. Terrible Owl was flittering around wickedly from bush to tree, hunting and pecking at thin air.

'Help me, here! I promise I'll help you!' the fox panted to the owl.

'You promised that before,' Terrible Owl crossly screeched, 'but he has got away!'

'Help me tie her with this vine,' the fox pleaded. 'Then I can help you catch him later. Four eyes are better than two.'

The owl agreed; they set to work. After Mrs Hedgehog was tied, the fox began arranging details. The owl got enthusiastic, too, about the prospect of Hedgehog Pie. Pleasant followed them and climbed in the brambles and grasses near the fox's place.

'I suppose it's a pity I'm not fatter,' said Mrs Hedgehog, trying to make conversation.

But the fox was busy with his cookery

book, replying nothing, for he was looking up instructions for making Sweet Sauce. It occurred to him that such a worrier needed a special sauce.

The fox may have known many small things; but Mrs Hedgehog knew one great thing, that she wanted to get out of there.

Terrible Owl, sitting on a low branch, hummed blissfully to himself and shut his eyes with pleasure. It was good to have a friend and to share with that friend.

Mrs Hedgehog did not cease worrying about her future. Pleasant, who was still hiding and waiting to be a hero – waiting for the moment to spring out and gnaw away the ropes that tied her – fairly danced in the grasses, limbering up his legs and making sure his rope-cutting teeth were sharp. He ground his white, white teeth together. The teeth made a strange noise – a sort of grating, or rasping.

'What is that?' asked the owl, whose

fortune depended upon the keenness of his hearing. 'It sounds very peculiar to me. Like the grinding of a pair of huge teeth!'

Mrs Hedgehog spoke. 'Maybe somebody is going to eat us *all* up now,' she said, with her usual worrying gloom.

The minute she mentioned it, it seemed quite possible.

Pleasant Fieldmouse kept trying his teeth, getting them razor-sharp for biting the rope.

Tired Fox and Terrible Owl looked at
each other with alarm, the cookery book was
thrown into the air with its pages fluttering;

then they raced off, banging into trees,
before they could be gobbled up . . .

Softly Pleasant slid up to the bound captive hedgehog, who thanked him after he chewed the knotted ropes loose, and he dashed off with her in the opposite direction.

While running they smelled the forest lilacs. Mrs Worry-Wind Hedgehog was spilling some grateful tears. 'They tell me not to worry,' she said sighing, while he accompanied her to her house. 'Well, some people have things to worry over.' She found the leaf necklace and put it on.

'Only fools don't worry!' she called out from her window, before she slammed shut the shutters.

Pleasant scurried back to his oak-home and locked the thick door. All night long he heard the owl and the fox passing to and fro, arguing and fretting and growing hysterical.

'Do you think we were tricked?'

'Do you imagine that slip of a fieldmouse went back home?'

'Mousie-wowsie, are you in?'

'Should we knock and ask?'

'Why didn't you forget about HER, when we almost had *HIM*?'

They went on quarrelling between them, but Pleasant muffled up his ears and dropped asleep.

In the morning there were signs of a fight not far from the fox's log – a few grey feathers and a tuft or two of bright red fur.

The canoe was gone again; they had made up and had paddled away together, taking a real trip for their health. Mrs Hedgehog, the next day, baked pies for everyone. All the forest favourites: dandelion, plum, daisy, apricot, chestnut, thistle. And that was the only kind of Hedgehog Pie that ever got eaten around *there*.

The Lucky Button

It was spring, yet one morning it turned cold.

Frost spread over the ground its icy crystal blanket. The season appeared to be going backwards. Pleasant bounced from his house, shutting his eyes and crossing his toes, saying,

> *Frost is not good,*
> *when you want luck in the wood.*

The tree limbs shivered. The rabbits and

43

chipmunks huddled inside deep holes. Even Greybeard Tortoise climbed back into his speckled shell.

'Well, you can't expect fine weather to run like clockwork,' Pleasant admitted, wishing he had a pair of gloves on.

Soon, however, he enjoyed frolicking upon the frozen turf and watching his tracks behind him forming solidly, just like they did in winter.

After a while – having tunnelled through a nest of sugary bluebells, scratching his way through the prickly bracken – he came upon the print of a monster-size foot. In fact there was a pair of prints, with a great many others ahead and behind. Some man-in-boots had stamped along here, probably searching for a short-cut to the lake.

Soon, most of the forest people gathered, trembling at the sight and smell of the tracks as much as from the sudden cold in the air. Mothers whisked their babies back home, for when men invade the forest, the animals must hide rapidly.

The fieldmouse moved on, hoping to make sure the footprints headed straight out of the forest, when he happened to find, sparkling in the brilliant morning glare, a button which had been torn off the jacket of the man-in-boots when he had passed a briar tangle.

Pleasant glowed with excitement: it was not every day you located such a magnificent, handsome button! So home he rushed and polished it at a furious tempo until it was glistening superbly. He sat studying it for a long, long spell, letting the light shine through the holes.

'I will call this button Charles,' he said. He had heard once (there was no reason why it couldn't be true) that some buttons have special powers.

'Look!' he ran around saying, showing it off. 'I've found such a lucky button!'

All oh'd and ah'd over the treasure, envying his stroke of fortune. At that moment the sun happened to burst out, shining extra hard – the last of the icy frost melted, the grass became fresh and green again, early flowers bloomed on their stems; and the thin ice crust over the stream was splintered into little pieces, so the ducks could freely paddle along.

'It must be the lucky button at work,' they agreed, and went away satisfied that the thing was pretty extraordinary. Everybody was too nervous to test its *not* being lucky.

However, Anxious Squirrel appeared then, in a dreadful state. He was twisting his furry tail on Pleasant's doorsill when the fieldmouse returned.

Pleasant Fieldmouse smiled, asking whether he was wanting to rub the lucky button?

'No, thank you,' replied Anxious in a very dramatic tone, wringing his paws together till tufts of fur flew forth. 'It's too late, for a squirrel who has LOST HIS MOTHER.'

'How in the world did you manage to do that?' Pleasant wanted to know, pulling up a couple of pieces of bark for them to sit on, friendly-like.

Anxious Squirrel stared straight into the sky as if he expected to read the answer high above. 'Mother trotted out this morning,' he said, 'just as she usually does for her trot after breakfast. Often I follow behind her. Then she shows me which berries are ripe and which nuts might fall next and where the sweetest water runs; and we practise high-leaping and tail-stiffening and so forth. But today I was cracking a nut apart – near the lake shore – and all at once she DIS-APPEARED.' The squirrel sat for an instant, letting that sink in.

Then he went on desperately, 'I heard that you had come upon the footprints of a man-in-boots, so I am fearing the worst.'

And he feared with good reason, because troublemakers though Terrible Owl and Tired Fox were, man becomes the very worst of troublemakers – with his big boots, his guns, and camp-fires.

Anxious glanced at Pleasant with a great deal of hope. 'Is there anything to be done?' he asked in a whisper.

Pleasant looked at the lucky button, Charles, for a moment, peering absently into the two tiny holes which were its eyes. At length he sprang upward, saying, 'We must *try*. No matter WHAT!'

So off they went in search of Mother Squirrel. The trail of footprints had melted, therefore they had to sniff and poke about and explore as best they could, crossing black circles of dark toadstools and other unlucky things.

The fieldmouse gripped the button in his paw as tight as he could, to keep it warm.

They pushed through a tangle of vines. And there they saw the man-in-boots, carrying Mother Squirrel in an orange-crate cage. She was scolding him loudly.

'Listen, Mrs Squirrel,' crooned the man-in-boots, 'you are going to be a pet for my little daughter Francie. And now you won't have to hunt for your supper anymore. Won't that be nice?'

No, Mother Squirrel did not think nice was the word for being locked in a cage or being dragged into town and treated like a toy. She thumped and pounded on the wire netting, protesting sharply. If you would like to know how Anxious felt, try imagining somebody taking your mother around in a cage.

Anxious was tying his tail in knots.

'Wait,' motioned Pleasant. 'Remember, I have this lucky button! I have a hunch I'm going to prove its luck now. We must slip in close behind the man-in-boots and not make any noise.'

They did, being still as grass without wind.

The man was bending low over the cage, which he had set on the ground.

'You must be hungry, Mrs Squirrel,' he said, though nothing could have been further from the truth, because his prisoner had had a big nut breakfast from her store of food left over from the autumn. Mother Squirrel was a handsome provider. Her son Anxious, however, had a bottomless pit for a stomach, and he had brought some nuts to nibble on during their morning trot that day, and it was while cracking his walnut-treat open that he had lost sight of her.

The man-in-boots was bending over,

withdrawing a piece of stale yellow cheese from his pocket. 'Here, Squirrelykins,' he said.

Mother Squirrel kept chattering, and turned away in disgust.

Pleasant Fieldmouse then scurried up, almost underneath the legs of the man-in-boots, pitching the lucky button forward. Charles rolled ahead, then spun to a stop in front of the man's left boot.

The man-in-boots glimpsed its glittery movement, immediately forgetting he had just that instant opened the door to the cage in order to hand the squirrel the piece of cheese.

'The button!' he exclaimed. 'The button to my jacket!' He made man's usual mistake of putting the less-important before the important, and reached out for his lost button. 'Now my wife can sew it on again like new!'

Since the door to the cage was ajar, Mother Squirrel took the opportunity to escape. Swiftly, swiftly she joined the field-mouse and her son, and they scampered off, all three, to safety in the bushes.

Mother Squirrel hugged her son with delight.

Pleasant skipped on his way with a cheerful heart before it was his turn.

The sun was dripping down with golden honey, and spring warbling birds poured their shimmering songs out from trees.

'Who doubted that the lucky button was lucky? Because a thing is lucky if you call it lucky,' Pleasant declared. And there was nobody around to deny it.

The Guest in the Rose

Summer's net was dropped upon the forest. The animals filled their baskets with ferns and daisies and bluebells and bursting puffballs.

Pleasant Fieldmouse was patiently growing a rose.

He had cared for it throughout the spring, feeding its roots, watering the thorny stem, and bit by bit its leaves uncurled, timid and green. When warmer weather came, the red blossom exploded slowly, the satiny petals stretching forth to catch the daylight.

Pleasant stood proudly by, shading it with an umbrella he had fashioned from odds and ends, whenever the sun became too blistery and hot. He watched the dewdrops slide off smooth petals, gracefully splashing on the ground. He held the umbrella devotedly up when a shower broke and fierce rain fell. He built a fence of stones around the rose bed for safety's sake – so Mrs

Hedgehog, or anybody else, in sleepwandering wouldn't unknowingly trample on it in the middle of the night.

It became a brilliant rose, and everybody clustered near to stand and stare.

They approached on tiptoe, admiring it. 'Don't make too much noise,' Pleasant would warn them – as if the rose were sleeping. Some of them even dreamt about it. It was the reddest, the most perfect rose ever seen.

If the wind blew, the fieldmouse would cover the rose with a screen, when the night grew chilly, he anchored the screen and closed the opening at the top with a blanket.

He watered it, and kept the earth around rich and black and artfully raked with lines like S's. The rose could not have asked for more.

However, one morning he awoke and donned his slippers and dashed outside to see how the rose was faring, and found, to his horror, it had turned a pale, dim red. The leaves were partly curled and dry.

As quickly as he could, he fled for the watering can to pour water tenderly over. It seemed to him he heard the rose sputter – not once, but twice.

'Have you had enough?' he discovered he was inquiring; he seemed to have grown a most strange rose.

He rubbed his ears when it replied, in a

distinct, half-drowned, tiny voice, 'Yes, I have!'

He had to sit on a stool to think about it.

'Shall I go away and leave you alone?' finally it occurred to him to ask.

'I wish you would,' the rose-voice answered. 'At times I prefer to be by myself!' This response nearly broke the fieldmouse's heart.

The petals moved, folding up, until the rose looked like a closed fist. 'Let me take my nap, after my bath,' it said. And Pleasant tiptoed away.

The rose and he had long conversations after that, from time to time, about no subject in particular, just things a fieldmouse might talk to a rose about.

Sleeping, eating, and drinking seemed to be the flower's favourite occupations. That was reasonable, because it was rooted there. Sadly the fieldmouse noticed the rose was turning paler day by day, despite his

attentions, until it had become quite pink –
as if all the life was slipping away.

'Are you sure you feel *healthy*?' Pleasant
would inquire with a frown. He loved the
rose a great deal.

'What a silly question! I'm plump and
very contented as I am,' the voice would
assure him, though the bloom appeared
straggly and lean.

Pleasant simply could not understand.
The others had long since stopped dropping
in – except to pause briefly, for a moment
only, clucking their tongues in a sympa-
thetic manner. They looked at the fieldmouse oddly, as if he must be having
headaches. But the rose really *did* talk to
him.

It was a very droopy-looking rose, getting droopier, and he watched it wither gradually away: the stem turning brown, the leaves peeling off like paper, the petals shrivelling.

Pleasant continued to feed it and water it every day, for he was a creature of duty and habit. It was mostly, now, the ghost of a rose. It leaned towards the ground as if it were bearing a great weight. The stalk began to fold in two, the pale flower would stagger with silent hiccups. The whole thing trembled. And one afternoon there tumbled out quite slowly a fat and sleepy worm.

Pleasant blinked in astonishment.

'Who are you?' he asked, asking Terrible Owl's famous question.

'Well, you ought to know,' the worm lazily answered, 'you've been taking care of me for weeks.'

The rose-watcher had to sit again. His legs were feeling wobbly.

'What do you mean, taking care of you?' was all he could manage. The rose was dry and shattered, the petals lay withered and black.

The sleek, lazy worm yawned.

'That was my nest – my house,' it explained. 'One night I crawled inside, and the rest I suppose I ought to thank you for. But I wonder if you might do me the favour of finding me another rose?' said the worm, idly stretching itself.

There was a long pause while the field-mouse tried to count up to five hundred. When he had counted as far as 377, he started laughing and gasping.

'Pardon me, worm, for getting angry almost,' he apologized. 'But you see, I was very fond of that rose; I thought it was talking to me.'

"Ah, I was fond of it also,' said the worm. 'The difference being, you wanted to GAZE at it. And – how should I put it?

It comforted me, giving me shelter. I think I got to know it much better than you. It made a cosy, sweet-smelling bed, and I regret having to give it up. I got to know every secret in it, while all *you* wanted was to admire its looks from the outside. I think it was *me* who loved it more,' the worm finished and burrowed down into the soil, flicking its tail before it disappeared.

'But it was you who destroyed it,' the fieldmouse insisted. 'By crawling inside! I

never would have killed the rose! I only wanted to admire it. I wanted to enjoy it, not to hurt it – I wanted it to live! That's why I fed it and watered it. You wanted to use the rose for your own selfish purposes!'

The drowsy voice of the fat worm floated up from the hole in the ground and then was gone like the rose itself: 'Maybe we'll never know which one loved it more!'

However, Pleasant knew, deep inside. He carried for ever the memory of that red, smiling flower which had bloomed, never asking anything but to give its beauty. He made a painting of it and hung it inside his living room, and the painting, at least, never faded, though it was not as good as the real thing.

A Forest of Ashes

Late one evening it stormed. At first, all the sky turned white like chalk. Everything stood still, holding its breath. Then a light shook in the sky and boldly struck. A peal of thunder roared and echoed far, sending everybody scuttling indoors.

Lightning flashed again, near by, on the other side of the stream. They saw a tree knocked down, split by a sudden bolt, bursting into vivid flames. Everybody sighed.

Mrs Hedgehog dashed away from her house to put up a lightning rod, though she realized, soon enough, she had nothing to construct a lightning rod out of. Now a stiff breeze blew, rising, it seemed, out from the bottom of the lake.

'Great! Great! Great!' croaked Never-Doubting Frog. He meant he hoped there was rain in the air.

Instead, a great bar of lightning came

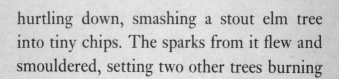

hurtling down, smashing a stout elm tree into tiny chips. The sparks from it flew and smouldered, setting two other trees burning (an oak and a maple); then these in turn ignited a beech, a birch, a fir, some delicate aspen branches, and a pine grove. There was a sizzling; next, wildly, flames burst out, and a sheet of fire and crackling grass brought householders to their doors. Frozen-faced, the forest people saw the forest they loved catching fire.

Running about in circles, families began fleeing. The fire appeared to spread forth in all directions: forward and backward, to the right and to the left. Where you least expected it to advance, it rushed.

The little tin warning bells of the field-mouse rang helter-skelter. Pleasant went scooting for his fireman's things. Haunted Beaver stood harnessed to the wagon.

Pleasant bravely stalked towards the fire. He alone did not panic. He waved his arms, crying, 'Here I come, ready or not! Watch out!'

He made gestures, swop swop, with his

swatter. The flames made horrible licking noises. Pleasant put on fierce and gruesome looks. He was attempting to scare away the flames, as he had done before.

The flames growled, making angry snarling faces back, showering him with ugly smoke.

He firmly stood his ground, shaking doubled-up paws. He was willing to wrestle the flames if it proved necessary.

'Hurray for Pleasant Fieldmouse, HE isn't afraid!' somebody shouted. But he almost *began* to be – his tail twitched a trifle – for he saw, to his surprise. the fire could not be scared. Yet this discovery did not discourage him much.

'Bucket brigade! Follow me to the stream!' he commanded. Most of the ladies, and all the children, were sent at once over to the opposite side of the stream where only one tree was left burning. The children played at putting that out.

In the middle of the forest the brigade was formed with Pleasant at its source. Pots and pans and acorn cups and every suitable container were used.

Water was drawn from the stream, hurried along to be splashed upon the roaring wall of fire. When the first flames were put out, a lot of people cheered, 'Hurray for our Firechief!' But other yellow flames rapidly grew to take the place of the doused ones.

A wreath of smoke surrounded the forest. 'Oh, I forgot to shut the windows!' Mrs Hedgehog said, worried as usual.

'That's all right, your house is burning down!' some neighbour informed her. And sure enough it was.

For a moment it looked like all the lamps had been switched on at once. Then flames shot through, turning Mrs Hedgehog's house into cinders, and then the cinders blew away.

'Don't worry, you will find a place with a better view,' Pleasant promised the suffering lady through the haze of smoke. 'After this is over, you will.' For he believed, from head to toe, that things cannot remain unpleasant. That when things are at their worst, you know exactly how bad they can be, and that they of course must get better.

So he closed his eyes against the raging fire, believing with all his might. He believed powerfully enough to move the clouds over the forest. Because at any rate buckets and buckets of water from the sky poured down, and a thick, splendid blue rain swished and battled against the hard-fighting flames.

Pleasant twirled his fly-swatter with joy and raised his cap in salute. Each flame sank unhappily to the ground and was snuffed out in a sizzle. . .

He lay on his back, drinking the rainwater. The next day a blanket of grey and brown cinders and ashes was heaped over the ground; unsightly charred stumps and blackened tree limbs were scattered through the once-green, once-beautiful forest.

However, Pleasant went straight to work directing crews of sweeper-uppers sweeping all the ashes away. He gave his helpers red bandannas to tie over their noses so they wouldn't sneeze and blow the ashes back.

Another crew went house-hunting and house-building, and though Mrs Worry-Wind Hedgehog worried that they wouldn't get her new one right, they did.

A great many birds, and the Squirrel family too, contributed seeds, while Pleasant ran his wheelbarrow back and forth, sowing pips, fruit stones, and seeds which would spring into bloom.

The mothers and children had saved most of the furniture by moving it across the stream. They even saved pieces belonging to Terrible Owl and Tired Fox, in case that pair returned from voyaging.

The sun slipped down, looking very much like some orange-and-red crushed rose.

And weary, but feeling that they had accomplished a great deal, they all went home to their new houses to have their suppers. The sweepings were being used as fertilizer around all the new-planted flowers and shrubs and trees. Next year the forest animals would forget that once the forest had been filled with ashes. The fire would be an old story when the dazzling colours came forth to surprise them.

A lark, who stayed up late, sang her song from a high bough. Pleasant lay in his grass hammock, listening to the golden notes, gently rocking. The song carried him upward over the fading clouds into the rainbow that was . . . and he dreamed of sliding down, down the shimmering rainbow into his soft, comfortable bed and maybe waking up and finding his house surrounded by a circle of small white mushrooms.

Also by Jan Wahl

THE FURIOUS FLYCYCLE

Melvin Spitsnagle was pretty popular at school – his father owned an ice cream factory – but he wanted to be liked for himself alone, so one day he asked his father to give all the unsold ice cream to an orphanage instead of to his school friends.

Nobody much came to see Melvin after that, so Melvin said 'Pooh Pooh!' to everybody and decided to spend his time becoming a scientific mechanical wizard in the unused barn he used as his private workshop.

Once he had achieved something that would make his bicycle fly, even his father admitted that his disappointing son was a satisfactory investment after all.

TOM ASS

Ann Lawrence

Poor Tom went adventuring to London with Jennifer as his companion. As the days went by he began to find her a better friend than he had expected, and to see that a donkey with two magic gifts might make his fortune yet . . .

A merry, magical tale, set in the England of old, when the bells of London town and the spirit of Christmas still wove their age old spell, and the Good People still thought it worth their while interfering to reward or punish the deeds of mortal men.

THE LAST OF THE DRAGONS
AND SOME OTHERS

E. Nesbit

'Why,' said Effie. 'I know what it is. It is a dragon like St. George killed.' And Effie was right, the winged creature that came crawling out of the boot really was a little dragon. In fact, there were 'winged lizards' appearing all over the country, though the newspapers of course never called them dragons, for fear of looking silly.

Indeed, as E. Nesbit cheerfully remarks, 'No one believes in dragons nowadays,' but by the time you have read a few of these stories you may be pretty well convinced – after all, if dragons *weren't* real how could the author know such a lot about them and the different ways clever people have outwitted them?

JAMES AND THE GIANT PEACH

Roald Dahl

James's life could hardly have been more horrible, walled up in a ramshackle house with his two beastly aunts. There were no toys and no friends to play with, and certainly no trips or treats; nothing but jobs, fetching and carrying, and being called 'you disgusting little beast' and 'you filthy nuisance'.

Then something magic happened. The fruitless peach tree in the garden grew one magnificent peach—luscious, beautiful and almost the size of a house! And one day James found his way into the interior of the peach, a strange little room which held a gigantic Silkworm, a huge Ladybird, a great vain Centipede, an enormous Old Green Grasshopper, an outsize but sentimental Spider, and a socking great sarcastic Earthworm. But all these creatures were far nicer than James's aunts and the adventures he had with them in the huge travelling peach were a great improvement on his other life.

By the author of *Charlie and the Chocolate Factory*.

A HARP OF FISHBONES
AND OTHER STORIES

Joan Aiken

Joan Aiken's books are a perpetual and delightful surprise, and this collection of brilliantly varied stories is no exception. There's the sad, spell-binding tale of Johnny Rigby; about tears locked in a heart and a heart locked in a river; the story of a confiding little ghost puppy; and a weird story of a baby whose cradle lay across the wolf's path, and what befell him. Harriet and Mark Armitage, the children with the pet unicorn, are here again engaged upon an adventure concerning a griffin's egg; and of course there is the fairy tale of the title about a little orphan called Neryn and the magic harp of fishbones she made in memory of her lost father.

MRS FRISBY AND THE RATS OF NIMH

Robert C. O'Brien

It was only five days now till the farmer ploughed up the garden and even the owl could see no way out, no hope of saving Mrs Frisby's delicate son Timothy from moving house in such dangerously cold weather. 'You must go to the rats,' he said.

The poor little mouse spoke with a sob in her voice, 'I don't know any rats,' said Mrs Frisby. But for Timothy's sake she went to visit the strange rats who lived under the rose bush, and learned for herself the secret that her husband had concealed from her for so long, the secret that made him and the rats of NIMH so uniquely different from other animals, and consequently put them in so much danger . . . .